PRAISE FOR

'Sometimes, Kassab shows us, love can be another word for cruelty. Sometimes the stories we hide behind reveal our deepest truths.'—*Sydney Morning Herald*

'Beautifully told in Yumna Kassab's poetic prose, *The Lovers* is both the story of the tumultuous relationship between Amir and Jamila and an exploration of class, culture and the complex nature of love.'—*Sunday Life*

'The delicate power that fables hold—their universality, while retaining their specificity—is captured in *The Lovers*. Ultimately, Kassab's novel rests on the premise of the "impossibility of language, of being able to ever understand someone else".'—Artshub

'Her writing is poetic and reverential. The author's understanding of love, romance and of responsibility runs deep.'—*Books+Publishing*

'a raw, haunting and honest look at love, relationships, and the moments that break us'—Mamamia

ALSO BY YUMNA KASSAB

The House of Youssef
Australiana

THE
LOVERS

YUMNA KASSAB

Originally published in 2022 by Ultimo Press,
an imprint of Hardie Grant Publishing.
This edition published in 2023.

Ultimo Press
Gadigal Country
7, 45 Jones Street
Ultimo, NSW 2007
ultimopress.com.au

A catalogue record for this
book is available from the
National Library of Australia

NATIONAL LIBRARY OF AUSTRALIA

The Lovers
ISBN 978 1 76115 317 4 (paperback)

Cover design Mika Tabata
Text design Bookhouse, Sydney
Typesetting Bookhouse, Sydney | Sabon LT Pro
Copyeditor Ali Lavau
Proofreader Camha Pham

10 9 8 7 6 5

Printed in Australia by Opus Group Pty Ltd, an Accredited ISO AS/NZS 14001 Environmental
Management System printer.

MIX
Paper | Supporting
responsible forestry
FSC® C018684
www.fsc.org

The paper this book is printed on is certified against the
Forest Stewardship Council® Standards.
Griffin Press – a member of the Opus Group – holds
chain of custody certification SCS-COC-001185. FSC®
promotes environmentally responsible, socially beneficial
and economically viable management of the world's forests.

Ultimo Press acknowledges the Traditional Owners of the Country on which we work,
the Gadigal People of the Eora Nation and the Wurundjeri People of the Kulin Nation,
and recognises their continuing connection to the land, waters and culture.
We pay our respects to their Elders past and present.

FOR IBN BENITO ALMAGRO

Let fate have its hand

CONTENTS

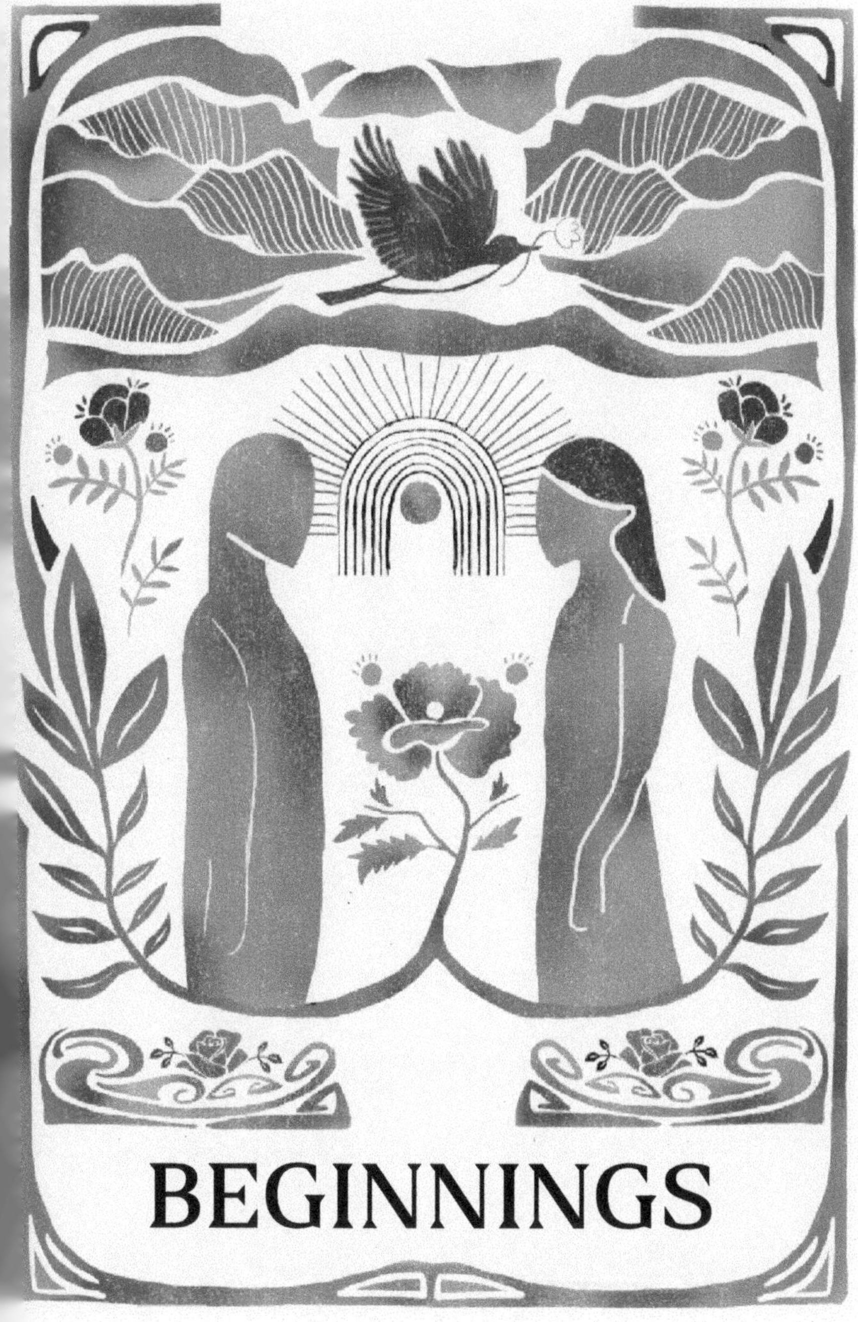

BEGINNINGS

THE OPENING

What Amir loved most about Jamila was that she smelled of money. There was the perfume she used at her neck and wrists, there was the cream she rubbed into her skin, there was the shampoo that cost more than he made in a week. She was always in a gown that was from overseas and she would open it to him and say, 'Come to me.'

He could have died a happy man beneath her love, believing himself an entrant to Paradise at last but had she been local, chances are she would have been unworthy of a second glance. Amir knew this as he caressed her, he knew this as they joked about a future in which a child of theirs was born. They bantered over devotion and eternity but he knew if she found herself carrying a child, she would deal with it as efficiently as her gardener tended the perfect lawn.

Women like her did not stay, women like her only joked until it was time for her to return to her home. At best it was a dalliance, a sweet pleasure to enjoy until it dulled and then she could pack up her things and follow whatever light her circumstances offered her.

He watched her and wondered how much time was left to them. Was it a week, was it a month, would they see out the year together before she tied her robe again, and left him with a decaying memory of a fragrance that was hers? He told himself he would leave before pleasure turned to suffering, before their romance turned to ash, but he knew he would stay as long as Jamila would have him, as loyal as a servant, panting over her like any old dog.

DELUSION

I absolutely love this place. That is what Jamila said.

And what exactly do you love about it? Is it the building missing its ear or its side? Is it the electricity that only comes on in six-hour blocks? Is it that people must live with their parents because they have no other choice? Perhaps it is that we can't trust our government so it is left to us to limp along as best as we can? Is it the lawlessness of the roads, that obey no rules of reason or logic that can be deciphered by a rational mind? Is it that families do not speak to each other for generations over a slight you would take in your stride? Or perhaps it is that a university education is to no avail and in the end you will live a farmer's life?

The people are so much happier here.

You say this about the person who is begging in the streets because that is the only way they can get by. You say this about the refugee, the child of refugees who were also born to refugees, stretching all the way back to 1948. They live in shacks that have no water, no electricity, their possessions in bags because tomorrow the government may move them on. You say it about the daughter who has none but her family to fall back on, who leaves with only the clothes on her back—even her children belong to the husband—and there is nothing to say she has the right to ever see them again. She is not happy, she has no future, she smiles because it is a reflex and she has been taught her lines so well. You say this about the one who agonises in his bed and then passes on suddenly because no one knew how sick he was. He was not peaceful but his disease was undiagnosed so it had no name and therefore did not exist.

I sense so much possibility.

You sense it because you are used to another life. You have money but will you sense possibility when your money runs out? Even if it does run out, you can take your suitcase, fill it with your things and return to that other country, and you can trust that between fortune and your government, the conditions are provided so you will prosper again. There is no possibility here, only that forced by people with their bare hands. The truth is we live like this because we have no choice, and if given a choice, we would choose to live our lives according to the pattern you live by overseas.

RAGE

Jamila was at breakfast. Her mother and aunt sat opposite her and they broke the conversation to have a bite. It was a temporary ceasefire and now was the time to regroup her troops. Her best defence was silence and to avoid their eyes. If her eyes met theirs, they would sense her uncertainty and redouble their attacks. It did not matter how many times they did this. Each time it was the house of cement collapsing on her head.

A woman with your possibilities, with your education, your wealth should not lower herself like this.

You could have your pick of men and you choose Amir who steals into your room in the night.

Don't kid yourself. He comes for your money, not your love.

And then the variations on this, tiny words changed, the order mixed up, their artillery launched onto her plate.

Lucy came in with a tray—milk, bread, fruit—and she had added rose petals because that was what Jamila had taught her to do.

She distributed the contents of the tray and then left, humming as she went.

Lucy herself had a love back home and when the time was right, she would let her family know. It would be simple, Lucy explained. The boyfriend was saving, together they would get a place, have some children, what more could we want?

Jamila thought of Amir, of how she used every weapon in the book to make him believe their love had a future, that—world aside—they had a hope.

Most nights he nodded his agreement, not because they were on the same page, but to keep the peace. She had the rage of a dragon. It made him fearful, it made him come alive. He kissed her and said, 'Be at peace. We still have the night.'

Her mother poured milk in the tea even though Jamila had repeatedly said she did not want milk in her tea. Jamila grabbed the tray and launched it out the window and waited for the crash. Then there was their silence and she decided it was time for a quiet cigarette outside.

FREEDOM

Once Jamila had believed that if she left, she would be free at last. So she left but she carried the stupidity of their world inside her.

Once she believed if she had enough money, they would leave her alone but no matter how high she built the fortress walls, they were family and they wormed their way in with a trick and a plea.

Once she believed she could move across the world and there at last she would be left alone. Alas, they followed her and said, 'Did you think you'd get away so easily?'

Once she believed in freedom but now it sits in a disused box. Not the United Nations, not the president, God or all the King's men had the power to intercede on her behalf.

ATTRACTION

Amir was not an attractive man. Even Jamila said it. And then she whispered, 'But I love you all the same.'

He thought of saying something that would shut her up, that would silence her for the rest of time.

Your ears stick out. A dentist could help you with your smile.

The words were on his tongue. They would have slipped out if it weren't for his restraint.

Anything he said would wound her ten times more than the words he'd heard from her. It was likely she wouldn't forgive him, that she would walk out. And perhaps the drama, the excitement, would be satisfying for a minute, but the effort to win her back would be too great.

So he touched her hair and said soft things.

He soothed her every night.

He counted her fury as charming, he made note of every time she laughed.

He called her beautiful and incredible and he felt her quieten at his side.

When she said to him, 'Without you there is no light in my life,' he thought, *But when you leave, I know I will want them to bury me alive.*

Better a thought than words where they would torment him, and her, robbing them of the flavour their time together still had.

PLAY

Samir invited the boys around for cards and they played till after one. He regretted that his partner was Mohammed who was the weakest player and together they lost round after round.

The night was getting on and Amir wondered about Jamila home alone. He thought about the wife he'd once had and the varieties of failure the universe can provide. Their families had smiled upon their marriage but if they had lived on an upper floor, he would have thrown his wife off the balcony.

Lucky there were no children. Lucky. Even these three friends said it. Some relationships are fated. Others operate outside the universe's control.

Mohammed lost them another round and Amir excused himself to go outside. When his wife went screaming to her parents' house, his mother said, 'You need to go get her. Her life is at your side.'

Why was it that she offered this advice so easily when it tripped him as if his ankles were tied? Amir retrieved her like a pet, like a suitcase, like a car that had been misplaced. She came willingly but that night, the boys knew better than to ask about his wife. Even their women had stayed away and avoided his eyes.

He remembered when the marriage was done how he played at Samir's house till the sun came up, how he smoked so heavily he couldn't breathe, how he cleared every memory of her until there was no evidence that once upon a time a wife walked on this floor.

Another wife, his mother urged, but the thought sickened him and he imagined a lifetime ahead—alone—and how in such solitude there would be satisfaction of a peaceful kind.

Samir was the one who called it a night, who told them it was time they went to their beds, that they could come around tomorrow at the same time again.

As he was leaving, Samir stood close to him and said, 'It's good to see you looking alive once more.'

He thought of those words as he drove away and he thought of visiting Jamila so late. He could walk through the gate that squeaked, that was a dead giveaway for the neighbour who spied.

It did not take him long to make up his mind and turn the car so that he would be with her when the sun next showed its face.

She was asleep when he arrived but she woke and patted the bed at her side. 'Where have you been this night?'

She welcomed him beneath the sheets and when she whispered in his ear, he smiled and thought, *This is paradise.*

Sunny was the one who called it a night, who told them it was time they went to their pods, that they could come around tomorrow at the same time again.

As he was leaving, Sunny stood [illegible] and said, "It's great to see you looking alive once more."

He thought of those words as he drove away and he thought of the long [illegible]. He could walk through the gate that [illegible] way by the neighbour [illegible].

It did not take him long to make up his mind and [illegible] that he would go with her when the sun [illegible].

She was asleep when he arrived but she woke and turned the bed [illegible]. Where [illegible]

She welcomed him beneath the sheets and when she [illegible]

[illegible]

NEUTRALITY

Capitalism is not bad. It depends how it's implemented. Communism is good, in theory, but people mess it up.

A nuclear bomb is neutral. It comes down to how it is used.

Their sentences floated over her head. They chased her down the hall. She ate them with her breakfast. She took them into the shower and pretended they weren't acidic as she bathed.

Sometimes she cried. Sometimes. Mostly she was silent. Mostly she stayed inside.

These words on the TV, these were the words in the books. Her head was a dreamcatcher pulling them to tangle inside her whenever she went outside. Lately she goes between people who say that religion is not all doom and gloom.

Religion is like a political system. Any issues are related to its misuse.

Jamila thought of her father beating her mother nightly. *It is written. It is my right as a man.*

She thought of women as the greatest soldiers of war, more than those who were on the frontline.

She saw the women she knew cooling their heels, then settling down to whatever life dished their way.

She considered the weight of fabric, considered the endless justification of history.

It is called peace but the truth is we are more often asked to submit.

Peace. Submission.

Pick or choose.

Her mother said this as she put a patch over an injured eye. *He is not a monster. Do not blame the crimes of man on our religion, which really means peace.*

Every night she dreams. It is inevitable, no?

They chase her, they drag her by her hair, by her feet, by whatever part of her they can reach. They laugh as they destroy her. *It is destiny. We are mere agents delivering on truth.*

It is a nightmare, it is a nightmare, she dreams and dreams, and even when she wakes, she knows she has not escaped.

PEACE

Amir stood on the edge of the mountain. Amazing. This mountain had stood over every day of his life and he had not noticed it before. It surprised him to consider an alternative life in which this mountain did not exist. Say he looked to the east—his eyes could see into the horizon—and for as long as he could remember, this mountain has been the companion to his hopes and dreams.

When he was younger, his parents talked about taking the car and making a trip of it. A caravan of cars, out for the day, breakfast, lunch and snacks so that they could find a spot on the side of the road and then spread out.

Someday, someday, and he had grown up and it had taken till he was a man possessed to abandon the day and head up to see what the mountain had to say.

The place he stands is rocky, the ground is unstable, but he has no recklessness in his heart. Jamila is the reckless one, the one who may drive her car off a cliff, who may take her grandmother's only cups and smash them on the floor. That is her style, not his, but she gave him the keys and said, 'Go for a drive.'

Go for a drive and there is so much to do.

Go for a drive, solitary, when I could be with you.

Go for a drive without knowing how the journey ends or even if it begins.

He brought nothing to drink, nothing to eat. This was an hour stolen away but standing alone, the sea blue as far as the eye could reach, he understood at last that his heart was at peace.

He wondered at Jamila trusting him with the car that was her pride and joy. It was the only one of its kind in the country and it was better suited to arriving at nightclubs than a trip to the mountainside. Over every bump he winced as the dust kicked up, he worried over how he would wash it before returning it to her. But for now he stood and breathed and when the hour was up, he went back to the car and drove leisurely down. In their town, people came out to watch, they noted who was at the wheel. He did not beep a hello, he did not wind down the window to wave and chat. He did not want to attract any more notice than he already had.

When he arrived at her place, she was sitting in the sun, her hair curled, her nails freshly done. She smiled at him as he arrived, she blew a kiss and waited for him to park. He came over to her, a thousand apologies on his tongue for the state of the car. He had rehearsed the sentences and the words needed only to be said.

Before he could speak, she pulled him to her—she was always like the sun—and said *I hope you enjoyed yourself* and after that, he couldn't remember what he'd meant to say.

[illegible] he would [illegible] returning into bed [illegible] nothing [illegible] and [illegible] when the [illegible] he went back [illegible] and the [illegible] down in their own [illegible] came out [illegible] they [illegible] who was at the [illegible]. He did not [illegible]. He did not [illegible] down the [illegible] anywhere [illegible]. He did not [illegible] than he already had.

When he reached [illegible] she was sitting in the sun, her [illegible] closely, she would [illegible] as he [illegible], she [illegible]. He [illegible] to her without [illegible] apologies on his [illegible] the state of the [illegible]. He had [illegible] the [illegible] to [illegible].

Before he could [illegible] she [illegible] to her [illegible] always like the [illegible] — and said I hope you enjoyed yourself and after that he couldn't remember what he'd meant to say.

TORMENT

Amir meant to love her. It was his intent. He would love her completely, he would love her like summer air. Everything he had would be hers on a platter and tell me, what is nicer than the ability to serve?

He brought his wife home like a treasure, he unwrapped her like a gift on their bed. He kissed her hair, he kissed her hands, he marvelled at her from night till dawn and then for the hours beyond.

If there was a lesson, it was that their love was not his alone. He could shower her with his love as if it were all the gold of the world, he could build her a palace with his bare hands but his love was not shared and like a puddle of water, given time, it would evaporate.

His great love was met with a war.

His affection was met with a bite.

His desire to serve her was mocked.

Her words were like weapons and down they rained, and he told himself he was unsurprised but the truth was their fights had not been in his plans. He kept away, he avoided her eyes, he steered clear of the room she was in, and he began to pray.

He asks himself why he resorted to prayer at such a time, he who had learned the rituals but never prayed genuinely in his life? With his prayers was the hope they go their separate ways, he on an alternative path, she to whatever lay in wait. The world was filled with examples of great love being extinguished by an anvil called circumstance or chaos, depending on your frame of mind. It was possible this would not be the rest of his life.

He extracted himself as best as he could but where there's breakage, there's damage, and although time heals, he knew he'd always bear her memory as a trace. She left without a goodbye and he believed he could now begin his separate life.

People urged him to women again, that relationships were prescribed as much as the setting of the sun, but he was spent, he was emptied, and he did not believe he could love again until he met Jamila in the summertime.

Some call it destiny but it does not matter how it is named. It had the feeling of ease, it had the weight of fate and it was a love only the heavens could have arranged.

MY LOVE SO YOUNG

Religion should not be transactional. *Dear God, give me this and I will obey. Dear God, I need an extra suit because this one is worn and in return I will pray double time this week.* He knows it is not meant to be like that but he finds himself praying and Amir wishes he could have known Jamila when she was young, before her face was lined and she touches the white in her hair and laughs, waiting for him to say it adds to her beauty anyway.

I want to have known her when she was young so I can understand.

He wonders what he will have to pay for the granting of this wish but never mind, they are both alive and she is so young but it is still her, make no mistake. The only difference is she smiles more and age has not yet begun to soften her shoulders and make them round.

He watches her and then raises a hand and calls out her name.

She stops. He is a stranger. She will not know him for another life.

He wants to say something to her, to tell her he understands, that she is the only one he will truly love but he is cautious about forcing the hand of fate, how a slight tinkering could alter the course of their lives.

She waits for him and he says *I am sorry, I thought you were someone else.* She continues on her way, his love so young, and he returns to his home and thinks *I am the luckiest man fate has played with since the start of time.*

SHARK DREAMS

Lately a shark disturbs her dreams.

She is by the sea and she is standing on the shore with her dress hitched above her knees. She wades in, holding her dress, watching the roughness of the surf, wondering why she doesn't go home. It would be easy. Walk home, change her clothes, then warm her toes, but she finds herself shivering, asking if this is the day she will drown, the day that danger edges closer to threaten her.

The waves buffet her and she releases her dress. It is pointless to hold it. In these conditions, she is going to get wet and she should be prepared to stand unprotected before the grey terror of this wintry world.

She has heard a rumour about a shark and she knows better than to believe a shark can be tamed, that she can do anything except tend it briefly, release it and hope she doesn't lose her nose or a toe.

She finds the shark lying like a dead fish on its side. Chances are it has already expired. She is weighed by her dress but she tries to use it to her advantage, tying it to the shark's tail and tugging it back to shore.

What does a shark need so it doesn't suffocate before the fireplace? She bathes it with warm water, she sings it a song, she calls it to breathe and take to life. Days of no response and she senses the futility of her actions. She promises she will only keep it one more day before she buries it outside but she can't bear to do so, not when she has run her hand over its body, not when so many nights she has cried.

She arranges the burial, she takes the shark outside. She wraps it in the dress that was a sign of the time she hoped before life proved her hope a lie.

She tells herself to begin, that the shark is dead, but she can't bury it so she leaves it in the grave she's made and walks away.

Always she wakes to a knock at the door and it is her love, carrying her dress and asking to be allowed again the warmth of the fireplace.

She finds [illegible] to begin [illegible] the clock [illegible] but the [illegible] she [illegible] of the [illegible]

and walks away.

[illegible] lover, [illegible] herself, and [illegible] to the [illegible] again

the [illegible] of the fireplace.

SILENCE

The greater the water she pours, the greater his emptiness seems. She had thought by now he would have been filled to the brim, that there would be a break but instead his demands grow and she now believes them to be without end.

He cannot satisfy her, he will never satisfy her, he should have left Jamila to other men.

He compares his ankle with hers and he wonders how such a small-footed creature could cause him so much pain. He holds up her hand, he envelops it in his own, and he wonders how defeat can be exacted with her as the tiniest dose. He stands by her—he hovers actually—and he is uncertain before her other men. He asks her about them and she offers them like pearls that will make him choke. Her transparency, her ease, these he counts as qualities he loves, but about her past, he wishes she weren't so free. He wishes she kept the details to herself, that she did not have this crushing capacity to share.

What can he give her, what can he offer, what can he do to make her promise to stay at his side for the rest of their lives? What is there? Is there his lack of money, is there his absence of knowledge about the world, is he to keep her with his ordinariness (because, let us be honest, she has her choice of men)? What is there? Are there the details of his past? Is there his family which is more dysfunctional than most? But here she disagrees. His family is no worse, no better than her own.

He wakes in the middle of the night and she asks him where he is going. He kisses her before leaving quietly into the night, thinking about the life he knew, the life that awaits, how he never outgrew his uncertainty. He has carried it with him and he is unsure how to shed this solitude that is more comfortable than a home. How is he to do this? How is he to leave his past behind so he can meet her somewhere to give her the kindness that she deserves?

There is him, there is the night, there are his questions and his only answer is the silence all around.

solitude that man or can [illegible] than a home. How a[illegible] ne to do that [illegible] [illegible] w past him as he call[illegible] after her into [illegible] her [illegible] that se[illegible] [illegible].

There [illegible] the quiet, [illegible] questions and his only answer is [illegible].

PLEASURE

He emerges from her bedroom, he knows not to what world. Hours he has drowned and it all started with her saying, 'Come, my sailor, let the captain teach you a lesson in ownership.'

Amir has heard stories of men driven mad by women, a woman taking complete possession and then refusing to release her hold, and he called such men crazy, inhabitants of the imaginary, creatures as unreal as fairytales told to children at night.

She whispers something in his ear, and he wonders if it is a dare, a challenge, a promise or all of the above?

He is afraid that these pieces will break asunder and he will be like Humpty Dumpty in the nursery rhyme. He will not worry. That is a trouble for another night. Instead he goes to sleep smiling, and he thinks of pleasure, its texture, how it is desire bringing love to life.

FEATHERS

It had been another night of cards. Samir served them their drinks, the ashtray on the table was clean, and there were the small snacks they didn't notice themselves eating. They kept a tally of winners and losers, the playing pairs to which they belonged, but they played for so many hours that he threw down his cards and yawned and said he was slowly going blind.

They laughed and said it was as good a time as any to have a break. Samir's children filtered through, swapping glasses, emptying the ash tray, and he asked them what else they had in the fridge, if there was something other than coffee and tea. He poured them soft drinks, they all agreed it was getting late, and Samir said that before they went he had a story for them.

And so the story went.

'Once—this was years ago—there was a farmer who wanted to keep a bird. He put together all the money he had and went to the market and bought himself the most beautiful bird. It came with a big cage and the seller told him if he fed the bird apples, it would begin to speak. "That is how I've trained her but I make no promises because she is unreliable like all the daughters of Eve." So the farmer took his bird home and he praised its colours day and night. He occasionally let her out, he had this fantasy she was a rich princess and one day she would let her song be heard. He fed her as many apples as he could afford but that bird never said a single word, so he became angry that he had been taken for a ride and all he had was this ordinary bird. Mind you, it had the most glorious colours and the seller made a point that the bird might not sing. The farmer knew deep down he had bought the bird for her colours rather than her words but if you see the same colours every day, you tire of them,

46

and suddenly you want to hear some words. He thought, *I have given her apples and now I shall ignore her and she can starve in her cage for all I care*, but he had the sense to leave the door open because he did not want her death on his conscience. He reasoned that he could explain to God her escape had been an accident, if a misfortune later befell the bird. And of course there was a misfortune. The bird became more and more miserable, she shrunk into herself and finally lost her feathers. The farmer was so furious he took the cage outside and he hoped to God that in the morning he'd wake and find he was rid of so miserable a bird. He got his wish in a way. The next morning, there was a woman frozen at the door of the cage, and he knew she had been the bird. So he did what we're all meant to do: he carried her to a quiet place and buried her in the ground, wondering why he couldn't be content with feathers, why he had also demanded the song. If only, if only . . . but this is an old story. The world giving you feathers, the feathers you prayed for, and then you discover what you really want is a song.'

They were silent for a second and then they made jokes about Samir and his story. 'Tell us more about the feathers of the bird.' 'You can play cards, you can even serve coffee but yours are the stupidest stories I have ever heard.'

Samir said nothing but the next night there were no jokes about birds, women, feathers, storytelling or anything else. Jouad's missing wife had been found in a neighbouring village and it was said she had been starved to death.

Samir let them play a round and then he said he needed to go to bed. They left silently and wondered about the stories, how fact and fiction both use the same words.

The previous night he went to visit Jamila. He had expected her to be home but she wasn't. When he spoke to her in the morning, she said she had been out with friends. She volunteered no other details and he thought no more of it until Jouad was found beaten so badly that his mother was inconsolable when she saw her son's face. It was nothing, he told himself, but casually one time he asked her what had happened to the baseball bat she kept by the fireplace.

'Some kids borrowed it. Who knows? Maybe one day it will be returned.'

Eventually Samir had them around again for cards and they stuck to games except when Samir was in the mood to tell them a story. Amir came to hate the stories, bracing himself for what he was about to hear, but he told himself they were only stories, to tolerate them, *push them from your mind*, and that was what he told himself each night so that he was peaceful enough to sleep.

SHAME

PART I

He wonders where Jamila's going with this, if this is an instance of letting a storm wear itself out . . .

'The first boy I loved, properly loved, did not care for me the same. I was driven to desperation and you would not believe the lengths I was driven to, how badly I wanted to impress, how I wanted him to want me above everything else in the world, but in the end, I couldn't make him or any of the others stay. Every single love died and I wondered if it was worth the heartache and the pain.'

'I dressed for him, I danced for him, I plucked myself till I was bare and there was nothing else I could do.

'Before I slept with him, I slept with someone else, learning tricks, wanting to torture him slowly on that bed but what was any of it really worth? It makes me sad to think of myself, so young, so full of desire, and how all I wanted was for someone with a bit of attention to spare.'

'This story repeated itself so many times till I was sick with the weariness of it, with these romantic defeats. I wanted no more, I wanted to wash my hands, to say enough is enough, but it is a game I like and I find myself returning again and again, stepping in to play. Would I change it, would I change what I did, who I pursued, who I allowed into my life? I find it hard to regret my life in this way. Yes, there was much pain, yes, I wanted to die, but at least I tried, I loved, and it made me feel so alive.'

'I wanted to tell you this. I wanted you to understand. For once in my life, I wanted to be motivated by promise rather than worry that the one I care for means to escape. I know I cannot make anyone stay. I know this. We all know this but tell me how much of what we do is logic and reason, how much is persistence in the face of contradictory evidence?'

'This is the first time I have told anyone this, this is the first time I have let my guard down in this way. It makes me fear where we might go from here but if I don't do this now, when will I do it? Do I grow older, older, hiding because of my very human fears?'

PART II

She wonders where Amir is going with this, if he will exhaust himself given enough time . . .

'I gave her everything. I would have given her my life if I could and all I wanted was something small, a nice word, occasionally a smile, but she was like a storm, constant, and there was no calming her down. It hurts later when people say *I told you so*, when they say that you shouldn't have wasted your time, that you were trying to give breath to a dead animal that cannot be brought back to life. What help is that to me? What good does it do for me to be reminded of this? Really I loved her and all the love in the world was not enough to make her smile just once in the morning and once before she slept in the night.'

'I told myself I will be this good person, I will be a good man, I will not be like those who seek to control the woman in their life but her behaviour honestly drove me near out of my mind. I couldn't eat, I couldn't sleep and I knew that nothing, absolutely nothing, would be enough.'

'I had this fear that another man would come along and she would run off with him. It was completely unjustified.

She was many things but she was not the type to play around. Still I couldn't shake this fear, and I thought, I will get my kicks while I can, I will have a woman on the side, and I went so far as to look around, but Samir, he pulled me aside and said, "If you can't love her properly, if she does not feel the same, then it is better each person goes their way, that you don't force yourself through a torture when you can have peace of a different kind."'

'We have gone far, we have come close, what is there that remains to be said? These hurts of the past will not protect us from the future, they will not protect us from being hurt again but we go forth in life, we dance as best as we can. This is the bargain we accept and it follows us from our birth till we breathe our very last breath.'

POSSIBILITY

Jamila considers the people around her. There is the family nearby, eating quickly as if in a race. There is the pair, a young couple, away from parental eyes for a moment. She remembers times like this when she stole away, how she still steals away, how her lover is a shadow in her life, how she denies the presence of permanency.

What happens once we become used to each other, once we become bored, once we anticipate each other's moods like the seasons cycled in a day? What happens when you are tired of me and I tire of you? What keeps us together except the routine of a child and the boundaries of marriage and the law?

She considers the waiter, a man in his fifties who places bread on each table, who fills up each cup until it almost overflows. In the time she has frequented this breakfast place, he has always been here. She does not believe he takes a day off. She wonders if he has a wife, children, and it is likely. She imagines them warming themselves in the evening by a fire. He probably starts at 6, giving him an hour to prepare before the first customers appear, then finishing at midday when the doors shut for the day.

There is an old woman alone. Her hair is uncovered and she wears four necklaces over her jacket. Jamila has seen this woman so many times they often say hello.

Jamila has come with Amir on the days he does not work but she tends to frequent this place alone. It is a ten-minute drive and the food is always the same. Her aunt reprimands her: the wastefulness of having breakfast out when you can eat as well at home, and she shrugs because we take nothing into the next life except our bodies and the weight of what we did with our life.

She asks for another coffee. The waiter serves her with a smile, he asks after her plans for the day and she gives him a vague answer, one that satisfies his question but gives nothing away.

She drinks this coffee slowly. She thinks about the day ahead, she thinks about the night with him that has passed. She studies the family and imagines herself breakfasting with him in this way, a child of theirs at her side or his, or maybe one each for them to tend to, to drive them up the wall. She considers it, wondering about the longevity of such a fantasy, if it will have any life beyond a day, if it won't be strained, if subjecting it to the regular strains of life wouldn't ultimately break the camel's back of love. She wonders if it's worth the risk, if the storms that arise will be storms weathered, if they can see them to the other side. Why can't we stay happy like this? Why is it the human condition to seek the greenness of spaces outside our current life?

She considers and her mind makes its turn. She wonders about discussing it with him, the one who insists repeatedly that she commit to a future, to know he wants to spend the future at her side.

She asked for another cushion. He were causing her...

THE LUXURY OF SUICIDE

Here suicide is a quiet thing. There is no drama, there is no outward yell. It is the sigh trapped inside that has been forgotten by the world.

Amir considers it. There is the one who swallowed poison and climbed into bed to die. There is the one who drove the truck off the cliff. The family insist it was an accident. There is the gun, the rope, the chair. There is the romantic version—Hollywood—where the mourners gather and they are allowed the solace of tears, and he considers the days of darkness that have been his, how he never considered jumping off a bridge, falling to the rocks at the edge of a polluted sea. He could lie down on the train tracks but the train has long since stopped running, and the fuel required to set himself on fire is fuel needed to keep his family alive.

When she lent him her car, he considered again the subject of suicide. It would be romantic, it would be a statement to the world, but he was in another place now and besides, the car was hers, not his, and the last thing he wanted was to inconvenience the one he loved who told him daily that she loved him too.

THE BOYFRIENDS

Um Bilal, we remembered her as a girl of fifteen even though she is well into her forties. We heard about that marriage overseas, the one that did not work out, and how a lesser woman would have retreated from life and waited to die, but eventually she returned here, and she brought with her a son, a boy of four or five, and she gave the vaguest answers about who had fathered him. We all asked but she never said anything that satisfied our curiosity. She lived with that boy alone above the bakery, and from that time she received men into her bed. Some said she did it for money, others said it was to battle the loneliness of the nights, others still that she was a light woman, not much upstairs, or else she would see how people called her every name under the sun, that when they were particularly spiteful, claws out and swiping, they said them to her face and even to her son. This son was not Bilal but another and I know for a fact that Bilal lived with his father overseas and you know how you sit in the night, the fire is low and the tongue a little loose, and we would wonder—all of us did—what sort of mother leaves her son overseas and then is able to hold her head up and speak normally to strangers in the street?

She left her son overseas.

The men, one leaves and then another takes his place, and don't believe for a second when they say they're her friends. Women and men, they cannot be friends, and it is better for them to make friends from among their own sex.

She has never become rich but her money over the years has stayed the same even as the country has declined. For a brief period, they say she stays alone, she bides her time, the wind will turn and then she will be visited day and night again. I always remember her at fifteen or as she is in recent years: in a bathrobe, her hair in curlers, her feet propped up on the balcony. She wears slippers and she shows their soles to the world. Her son is grown and he has children of his own and he visits his mother daily, he brings her fruit, he brings her plates of food that his wife has cooked, and I heard the other day that maybe she no longer receives men because she's done using them, that she has no need anymore for them, that her son is all grown and he is taller than the men around him who look up to him from within his shadow, that he can now support her as she ages, that if she wants she can retreat from the world, she can hide and watch television all day and paint her nails in the sun as a woman of leisure as all women hope to be but come now, the mind is tired and the fire burns low so let us turn to our own lives, their failures, their hopes, and how no matter the stakes, we bear the darkness willingly because God promises us in the morning it will be light again.

NOCTURNES

She is calling the one she loves.

There. It is out in the world.

She lets the phone ring.

She is armed with an excuse, a reason for the call.
I need to check the homework for maths. Truth be told,
people call her to check but he does not know that.

That first love, how they snuck around. The illicit
catch-ups, their meetings carefully arranged: the notes
passed, the plotting and planning as if they were complex
strategists and the fate of the world was at stake.

She thinks of the girl she had been and her profound silliness and how she is sneaking around with him.

Amir visits her bed and then he leaves. Everyone knows it but none dare speak of it. To speak of it is to take it out of the night-time and air it in daylight, to legitimise it, to give it life, to say to the world *I may well be serious about this one,* to subject their young love to scrutiny, to comparisons, to turn it into a house of glass for the stones others throw with indifference or intent. She could not bear that, not at this early stage.

He asks her to marry him and she resists. She tells him he is joking, that he can't be serious, and he repeats he means the words that he has said.

She thinks of marriage, she thinks of being bolted to the ground, of being stuck to the floor, and she tells herself that with him it will be different but isn't that the line everyone the world over feeds to their self? He calls it her western cynicism, that with him there is no need for a mask, that he wants her in his life, that he will not let her go, that he does not care what anyone thinks.

That is how it always starts, she mutters and thinks of how hopeful she has been, rolling up her sleeves to greet each beginning with hope and how each time it had been cut down, of how many loves have died despite all her energy, her will and intent.

And what is there except a hope that this one will not go the way of the others and die a premature death?

It is a hope, nothing else. Upon it, the world turns, the axis of the globe, its tilt, and she wonders if she is willing to enter the ring again, to stake it all on a hope, a promise of something else but as he said to her: *Tell me, is there anything else?*

DUTY

The doubts are the worst.

Amal is telling her story—*he hit me just then*—and all Jamila can think is *here we go again*.

The doubts?

There are no bruises, Amal always has a smile on her face. If things are so bad, why hasn't she left? Surely it's not as she says. Come on, there is the door and no one is standing in her way.

But as a good friend, she listens, she nods often, she does not roll her eyes. As a good friend, she offers tea and biscuits, she offers tissues—here come the tears like clockwork—and she agrees that he is to blame for Amal's pain.

It takes an hour to calm her, to farewell her, to breathe a sigh of relief, ignoring the fact that in a week they will be revisiting the same mess that is the soundtrack of Amal's marriage. She is grateful it is someone else's lot in life, that she can wash her hands of it and consider her social duty discharged, making a decision about how to do her hair and the clothes she wants to wear.

She has tossed and turned over this subject at night. *How can I be a better friend? What else can I do to help her other than offer bandaids and painkillers after the beast has whipped her again?*

It is not my place, she tells her reflection, *she must sleep in the bed she has made, didn't she choose to marry him when we all shook our heads?*

What else can I do? she wonders, transferring a pin from her mouth into her hair, *I offer her shelter every time, I listen to her, I give her advice, I remind her how to make her life bearable, but the horse has been led to water and I can offer nothing else.*